THE CALM INSIDE

Written by
Ryuu Shinohara & Kate Moro

Ilustrated by
Hanna Musaliova

Copyright 2024
The Calm Inside: Inspiring Stories & Activities to Manage
Big Emotions, Stay Present, and Find Calm Peace - Adventures of Benny, Kiki, and Sam
Text © 2024 by Kate Moro and Ryuu Shinohara
Illustrations © 2024 by Hanna Musaliova
All rights reserved.

No part of this publication may be reproduced, stored in a retrieval system, or transmitted in any form or by any means—electronic, mechanical, photocopying, recording, or otherwise—without the prior written permission of the publisher, except in the case of brief quotations embodied in critical articles and reviews.

Disclaimer
This book is intended for educational and entertainment purposes only. While the mindfulness techniques and practices presented are inspired by general well-being principles, they should not be considered a substitute for medical or therapeutic advice. Consult a qualified professional for personalized guidance regarding mental or emotional health.

First Edition
Printed in the United States

Credits
Publisher: Omen Publishing LLC
Layout: Kate Moro
Illustrations: Hanna Musaliova

Acknowledgments
Thank you to everyone who has supported the creation of this book. Your belief in teaching mindfulness and joy to young readers has been invaluable.

THE CALM INSIDE

Inspiring Stories & Activities to Manage
Big Emotions, Stay Present, and Find Calm Peace

The book you're holding in your hands is part of the **Little Lessons of Mindfulness** series—a project with the mission to help kids build confidence and clarity by nurturing their awareness, thoughts, and emotions.

Introduction:

The Little Lessons of Mindfulness series is designed to teach mindfulness and universal values to children ages 4 to 8 through engaging stories inspired by Buddhist teachings. In today's busy world, kids face so much happening around them, which makes it harder to stay calm and focused. This series aims to provide a foundation to help children learn, develop, and apply techniques that support them in managing their thoughts and emotions and in overcoming life's challenges.

Each book focuses on a core theme to help young readers build essential qualities like focus, empathy, courage, and more.

Here's a sneak peek into the journey this series will take your child on:

Book 1: The Calm Inside
Adventures of Benny, Kiki, and Sam
Inspiring stories to manage big emotions, stay present, and find calm peace.

Book 2: The Focus Inside
Adventures of Momo, Lily, and Marley
Engaging tales to improve focus, clear the mind, and build concentration.

Book 3: The Love Inside
Adventures of Ellie, Toby, and Roxy
Heartwarming stories to develop honesty, empathy, and caring.

Book 4: The Joy Inside
Adventures of Ziggy, Paul, and Sunny
Uplifting stories to build courage, spark joy, and embrace gratitude.

And more to come!

Together, this series creates a foundation of mindfulness, resilience, and positivity that kids can carry with them as they grow.

The Importance of Mindfulness:

Life can get a little wild sometimes, even for kids. One moment, everything's calm, and the next, it's a rollercoaster of big feelings! That's where mindfulness comes in. It's like a toolkit that helps kids stay cool, focused, and steady when emotions run high. Mindfulness teaches kids to slow down, pay attention to their feelings, and take a deep breath before letting those big emotions take over.

In this book, your child will join Benny the Bunny, Kiki the Koala, and Sam the Sloth as they each discover their mindful way to handle life's twists and turns. Whether it's keeping calm in a storm, staying focused on a goal, or slowing down to enjoy each moment, these gentle stories show that mindfulness can be simple and fun.

Through Benny, Kiki, and Sam's journeys, kids will learn how mindfulness can help them feel calmer, more confident, and ready to take on life's little ups and downs. And as they explore the world of mindfulness, they'll build focus, grow kindness, and find joy in every moment—one peaceful breath at a time.

How to Use This Book:

This book is not just for reading—it's for reflecting, imagining, and growing! After each story, you'll find special reflection questions designed to help your child think about the lessons they've learned and how they can use those lessons in their own life. These questions invite your child to imagine themselves in the story, think about how they would react, and explore new ways to manage emotions.

Each story also includes a simple, kid-friendly lesson that wraps up the main message of the story, followed by a fun exercise or activity to help your child practice what they've learned.

The best time to read this book? Anytime! It works beautifully as a bedtime story to help your child wind down and relax, or during quiet moments in the day when they need a little calm or encouragement. Each story brings a moment of peace and learning, creating the perfect opportunity to bond while teaching important life skills.

Your Exclusive Bonuses Await!

We're thrilled you've joined Benny, Kiki, and Sam on this mindfulness journey! To make the experience even more enriching, we've prepared some special bonuses just for you:

- Book & Meditation Audio

Listen along to the beautifully narrated audio version of the Adventures of Benny, Kiki, and Sam. Plus, enjoy soothing meditation tracks that guide your child through the embodiment visualization exercises. Perfect for bedtime, quiet time, or anytime you need a moment of peace.

- Coloring Printouts

Bring the adventures to life with our printable coloring pages! Featuring Benny, Kiki, Sam, and their friends, these pages offer a creative way for kids to relax, reflect, and have fun while reinforcing mindfulness lessons.

- Beta Readers Group Access

Be part of our exclusive beta readers group! Get sneak peeks of upcoming books and activities, share your thoughts, and even have a chance to receive new books for free.

Ready to unlock your bonuses?
Scan the QR code to access all these amazing resources!

Table of Content

Mission 4

Introduction 6

The Importance of Mindfulness 8

How to Use This Book 9

Your Exclusive Bonuses 10

Story One 12

      Lessons & Exercises 24

Story Two 26

      Lessons & Exercises 38

Story Three 40

      Lessons & Exercises 52

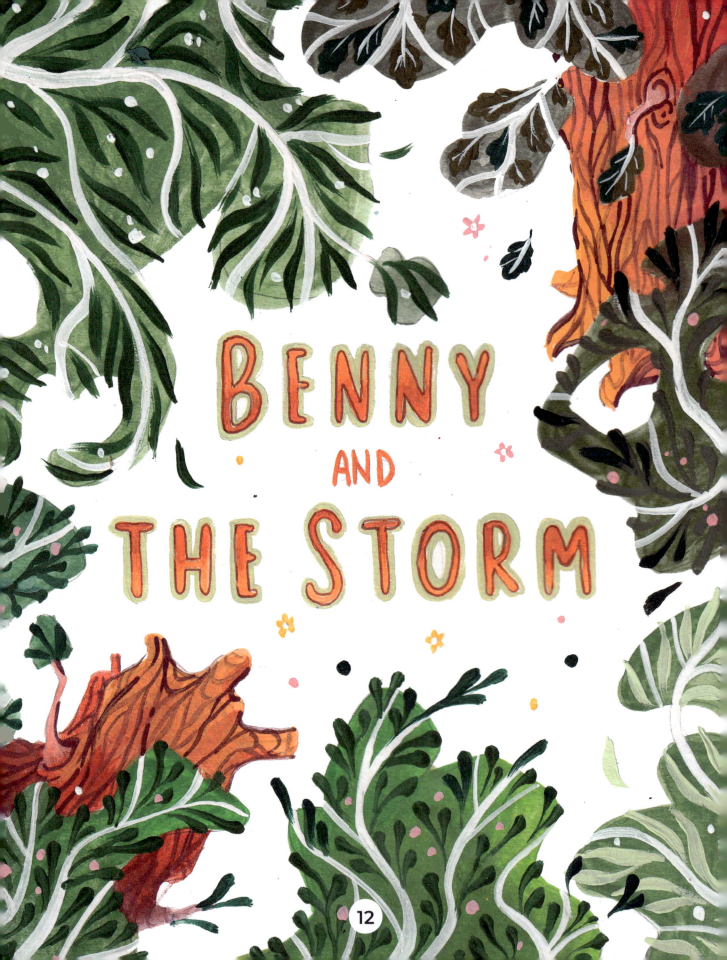

Relaxed. Peaceful. Calm. This was the vibe Benny the Bunny was on. He was the coolest, most laid-back bunny in the whole forest.

Benny had many tricks under his sleeve to stay calm and collected no matter what happened. What do you think these tricks are? Let's hop into the story and find out!

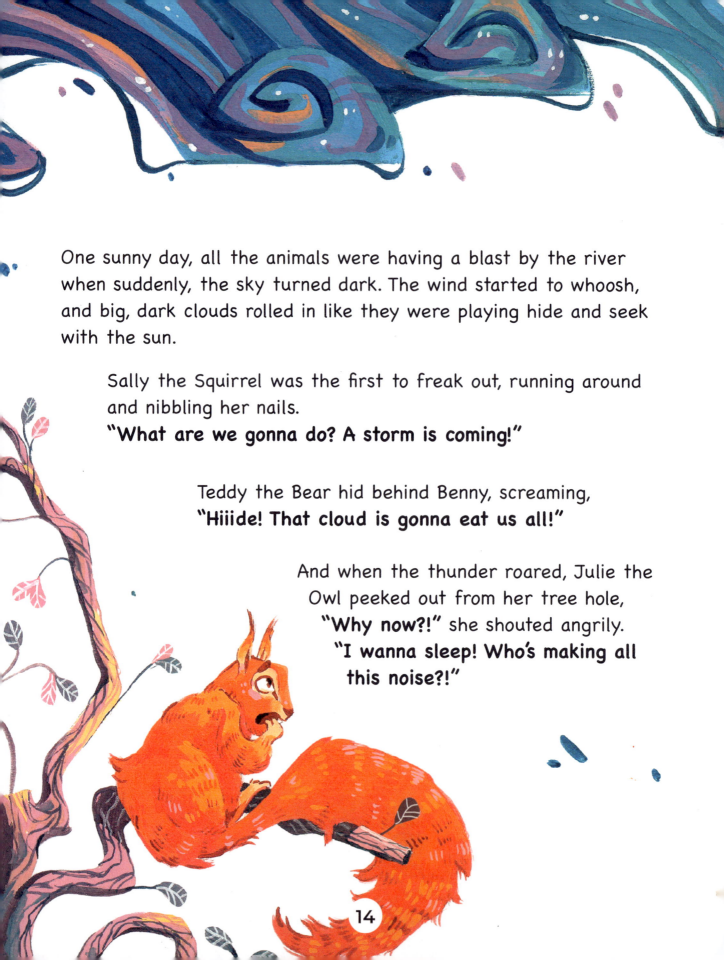

One sunny day, all the animals were having a blast by the river when suddenly, the sky turned dark. The wind started to whoosh, and big, dark clouds rolled in like they were playing hide and seek with the sun.

Sally the Squirrel was the first to freak out, running around and nibbling her nails.
"What are we gonna do? A storm is coming!"

Teddy the Bear hid behind Benny, screaming,
"Hiiide! That cloud is gonna eat us all!"

And when the thunder roared, Julie the Owl peeked out from her tree hole,
"Why now?!" she shouted angrily.
"I wanna sleep! Who's making all this noise?!"

The forest was in total chaos. Benny just stood there, watching his friends run and bump into each other. He knew he had to figure out how to fix this mess before things got even crazier.

"**Everyone, stop!**" he called out, standing on a little hill.
"**Let's calm down together.**"

First, Benny went over to Sally the Squirrel.

Sally was running around her tree like a whirlwind and didn't know what to do.

"Sally, no need to panic. Just close your eyes and picture your favorite happy place where you feel super safe."

Sally listened to Benny and did what he said, imagining herself relaxing on top of a giant tree filled with nuts of all shapes and sizes. Pretty soon, her panic faded, and her heartbeat slowed down.

Then Benny went to Teddy the Bear, who was shivering inside his cave.

"Teddy, I know you're scared, but let's take a deep breath together."

Benny gathered all his friends, and they started doing breathing exercises. One breath in like you're smelling flowers. One breath out like you're blowing out birthday candles.

When everyone was feeling much better, Benny turned to Julie the Owl. **"Julie, whenever you feel angry, try to turn that energy into something fun. Imagine you're dancing in the rain, letting the storm's rhythm guide you."**

Julie gave a happy hoot, spread her wings wide, and spun around, releasing all her frustration. With a smile, she felt calmer and drifted back to sleep, knowing how to let go of her anger.

When all the animals were calm, Benny said, **"Now that we're all chill, let's find a safe spot."** They all hid in Teddy the Bear's cave, listening to the rain patter on the leaves. They told jokes, ate honey, and played fun games all night long.

And before you knew it, the storm was over. The animals came out of the cave and were thrilled to see a beautiful rainbow in the sky.

"See," Benny said, **"storms come and go. But what's important is how you react to them. Whenever you feel worried, scared, or angry, remember you are the boss of your emotions."**

And so, with Benny's help, the forest animals learned to stay calm and enjoy the beauty after the storm.

LESSONS:

- Stay calm. When you panic, it's hard to make good decisions.
- Storms come and go. Find peace and wait for them to pass.
- When you're angry, release the energy in a positive way.

EMBODIMENT:

Close your eyes and imagine you're Benny the Bunny during a storm:

The sky is dark, and the wind is howling, but you stay calm. You take deep breaths, smelling flowers and blowing out candles. You find a cozy spot and think of happy places, like a snug cave with your friends. You feel calm and in control.

EXERCISES:

Safe Place Exercise

Close your eyes and take a deep breath. Now, imagine a safe place that makes you feel happy and peaceful, like Sally the Squirrel's mountain of peanuts.

What is your safe place?
Where is it? What does it look like? Is someone with you?

Mindful Breathing

Close your eyes and picture yourself as Teddy the Bear. Breathe in like you're smelling flowers and out like you're blowing birthday candles. Count to 10 or until you feel calm.

When could you use this exercise in your day?

Energy Release Activity

Instead of letting your anger out on others like Julie the Owl did, channel that energy into a light physical activity.

What's your favorite way to release energy?

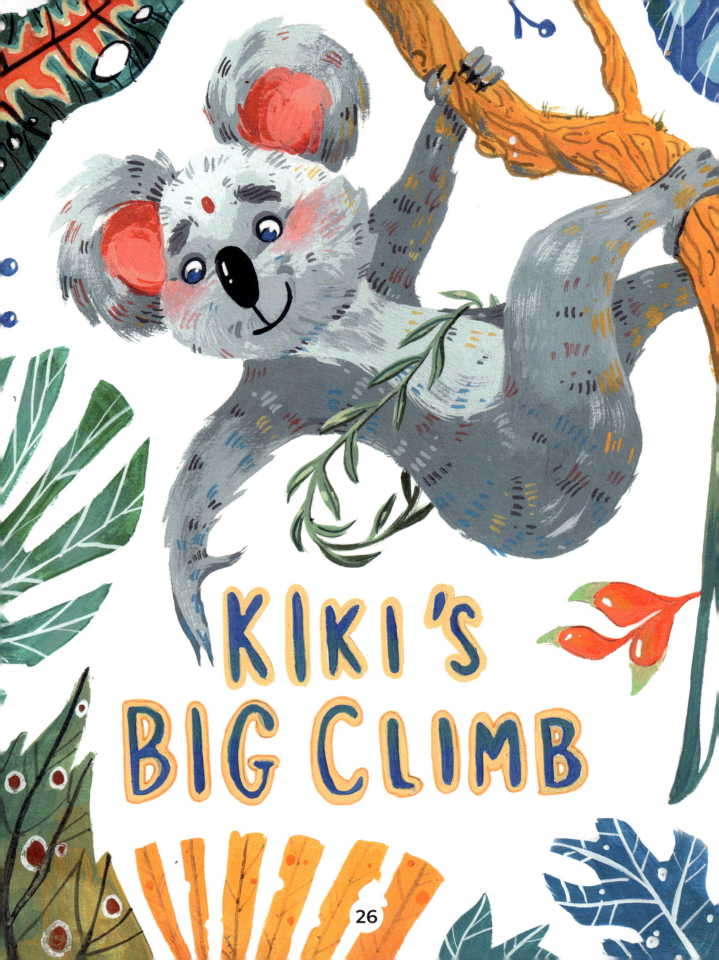

Way up high, at the tippidy top of every tree, lived the koalas. Koalas are known for being great climbers! With their strong arms and legs, they can climb up almost any tree.

One of these koalas was named Kiki. Kiki had a big dream—she wanted to climb the tallest tree in the whole forest, a tree no koala had ever climbed before: **the Infinity Tree.**

But every time she thought about it, she got tangled up in worry.

"What if a storm blows me off the tree like a balloon? What if I get so tired, I flop like a pancake? It's too high. No way I can do it," Kiki would think.

Do you think Kiki managed to overcome her fear and climb the tree? Let's dive into this story and find out together!

One day, while Kiki was looking up from the bottom of the Infinity Tree, along came Momo the Monkey, swinging from branch to branch.

"**My grandpa was like, the best tree climber ever! He always carried this blue bandana that reminded him to be brave,**" Momo said with a grin.

"**He always said the secret to climbing is to stay present and focus on one branch at a time, like you're playing a game of follow-the-leader. Just let each branch show you the way to the next one.**"

"**I'm thinking about climbing the Infinity Tree. Do you think I can do it?**" Kiki asked, her eyes wide.

"Totally!" Momo nodded. **"You have it in you; koalas are great climbers!"**

Suddenly, Kiki felt as brave as a knight. She took a big, deep breath and started climbing. As she climbed, she focused only on the next branch to lead the way—ignoring all the silly stuff around her, like wiggly spiders and fluttering butterflies.

As Kiki climbed higher and higher, those pesky fears started sneaking back in. But then she spotted Zazu the Toucan, chilling on a branch.

"I wish I could be as calm as you, Zazu," Kiki said with a sigh. "But I keep thinking something terrible's gonna happen, like the branch breaking or me slipping off."

"Your fears are just like shadows—they're not real," Zazu said. "Don't let them ruin your fun. Instead, think about what makes you feel happy and safe!"

Kiki decided to give it a try. Whenever she felt scared, she imagined Zazu swooping down to catch her like a superhero in a cape.

And before she could blink, Kiki reached the next big branch, where she plopped down for a break. There, she saw Julie the Owl doing yoga on a fluffy mat. Her nest was zen, filled with candles and singing bowls.

"Why do you need all this stuff?" Kiki asked, scratching her head.

"It helps me stay in touch with my senses," Julie said, stretching her wings.

"Hearing the singing bowls, feeling the soft mat, and smelling the candles brings peace to my heart. It keeps my mind from worrying."

Kiki liked Julie's idea. She wanted to feel peace, not fear. So she tried it out.

As she climbed higher, she focused on the sound of chirping birds, the incredible view of the forest that looked like a giant green carpet, and the fresh smell of tree bark. During her breaks, she munched on tangy berries while letting the cool breeze tickle her cheeks.

Each step felt lighter, and her fears seemed to drift away, like leaves on the wind.

And just like that, Kiki found herself at the very top of the Infinity Tree! Her heart swelled with joy, knowing she had faced her fears and won.

The worries that had once seemed so immense now felt like tiny pebbles at the bottom of the tree. She took a deep breath and smiled, feeling a sense of peace wash over her.

Sitting there at the top, Kiki felt like **the queen of the forest**. She realized that sometimes, you only need a little mindfulness and courage to reach new heights.

LESSONS:

- Mindfulness helps you stay present and focus on what you're doing.
- Paying attention to what's around you brings peace and calm.
- Most fears and worries are just things our imagination makes up.

EMBODIMENT

Close your eyes and imagine you're Kiki the Koala with one big mission—to reach the top of the Infinity Tree.

The **"what ifs"** are buzzing, but you're brave and keep climbing. Feel the cool breeze on your face and the rough bark under your hands. Hear the birds chirping and taste the yummy berries. As you reach the top, you feel calm, happy, and proud of yourself, enjoying the amazing view.

EXERCISES:

One Step at a Time:
Close your eyes and imagine you're Kiki climbing a big tree. Instead of thinking about how high the tree is, focus on just the next step. Picture yourself holding onto the branch in front of you, feeling the tree bark, and hearing the birds sing. Take one step at a time, just like Kiki did!

What's something big that you want to do but feels a little scary? How can you take it one step at a time? (like cleaning your room, reading a book, doing homework)

Senses Awareness:
Another way to clear busy thoughts is to focus on what's around you. Paying attention to your senses helps you stay in the moment and feel calm. So whenever you're nervous or worried, try to focus your mind on what you see, hear, feel, smell, and taste.

What are five things you see?
What are four things you hear?
What are three things you feel?
What are two things you smell?
What's one thing you taste?

PICNIC TIME WITH SAM

YAAAAAWN! Sam the Sloth stretched his long arms. **"What a fabulous day for an outdoor picnic!"** he cheered, rubbing his eyes.

Sam the Sloth was the best cook in the jungle! He was famous for his tasty food and love of savoring every moment.

While the whole jungle zoomed around like race cars, Sam always took his time, whether he was soaking up the morning sun or munching on a juicy mango before bed.

But the big question is: with his wacky friends around, would Sam be able to stay calm, or would their whirlwind of energy sweep him up? Let's swing into the story and find out!

Sam invited his best buddies for a picnic: Rico the Raccoon, Momo the Monkey, and Sunny the Red Panda.

As Sam chopped fresh veggies, they all bounced around like popcorn in a microwave, their eyes sparkling with excitement.

They could hardly wait to dive into their favorite treats: jungle omelet, Amazon salad, and mouthwatering banana cake.

Once everything was ready, Sam spread out a super soft picnic blanket, laid out colorful napkins and plates, and even decorated the blanket with flowers he'd picked with lots of love.

With a big smile, Sam closed his eyes and said,
"Thank you, yummy food!"

His friends' eyes were as wide as saucers, eagerly waiting to dig in. And when Sam finally said, **"Here you go, my friends! Enjoy,"** the hungry gang dove into the spread with glee!

They started shoveling the food into their mouths so fast, you'd think they were in a food-eating contest!

But instead of enjoying it, Sunny started choking on leaves bigger than her head. Momo was swinging around, scattering crumbs everywhere and making a huge mess. And Rico stuffed himself so much, he looked like a balloon ready to pop!

"**Hey, guys,**" Sam finally said, "**if you keep going like this, you're gonna end up with a serious tummy ache.**"

"**Too late, I already have one,**" Rico groaned, rubbing his round belly like it was a basketball.

"**That's because you're not really enjoying your food,**" Sam said with a gentle smile. "My granny used to say, 'Take it slow so your tummy will glow.'"

"**Huh?**" Momo scratched his head.
"**What does that mean?**"

"**It means everything starts before you even dig in,**" Sam explained. "Thank your food and show it some love. That way, you connect with what you're eating."

Then Sam showed them how to focus on their meal.

"To truly enjoy your food, be present with it. No TV, no books, and definitely no swinging around. Just you and your tasty meal, bite by bite, nice and light."

And last but not least, Sam reminded them to chew slowly. **"Think about every bite, and you'll see how much yummier it gets!"** His friends followed his advice, and the rest of the meal turned into the best feast ever.

They chewed slowly, savoring every single bite. The salad leaves became juicier, and the banana cake tasted sweeter than ever. When they finished, without any tummy troubles or overstuffed bellies, they all went back to playing together, feeling super happy and full of energy.

By the end of the day, Sam's friends realized that slowing down made everything better. Not only did the food taste amazing, but they also felt happier.

From that day on, they promised to always eat like Sam—mindfully, with gratitude, and at a pace that let them enjoy every moment. Sam smiled, knowing his friends had learned an important lesson: sometimes, the best way to enjoy life is to take it slow and savor every little bit.

LESSONS:

- Being mindful means paying attention to what's happening right now, so you can enjoy every bit of the moment.
- Being aware of how your body feels helps you eat at a pace that's right for you.
- Saying **"thank you"** before and after eating helps you really enjoy your food and the fun of mealtime.

EMBODIMENT:

Close your eyes and picture yourself as Sam the Sloth on a special picnic:

You're sitting on a soft, fluffy blanket with the sun shining and the air filled with sweet smells. Take a deep breath—mmm, can you smell the yummy food? Before you eat, you smile and say **"thank you."** You pick up a piece of banana cake, take a slow bite, and let the sweetness fill your mouth like a little burst of joy. Each bite feels special, and you feel as calm and happy as a cloud floating by. Can you feel it?

EXERCISES:

Mindful Eating:

Mindful eating is all about paying attention to everything about your food, like how it looks, tastes, smells, and feels. Taking your time and using all your senses helps you feel more connected to your food and your body. Pay close attention to how your body feels so you know when you're full and don't end up eating too much.

What's your favorite food? What does it taste like? What does it look like? What signals does your body give you when you're full?

Gratitude Practice:

After every meal, remember to say **"thank you"** to your food. The more you appreciate what you eat, the tastier it will seem!

Can you think of three things you loved while eating your meal? Maybe how good it tasted, how yummy it smelled, or how happy it made you feel?

A Short Message From the Authors

Thank you for joining Benny, Kiki, and Sam on their mindfulness adventure! We hope these stories have brought a sense of calm, peace, and valuable lessons to your child's life. If you and your little one enjoyed Book 1 of the Little Lessons of Mindfulness series, we have a small favor to ask: **Your review makes a big difference.**

By leaving a review, you're not just helping us improve and create more heartwarming, impactful books—you're also helping other parents discover tools that can nurture mindfulness in their children.

Together, we can spread this message far and wide, helping more kids learn to manage their emotions, find peace in the moment, and grow into confident, mindful individuals.

Here's how you can help
Scan the QR Code to leave a short review on Amazon.

We're deeply grateful for your support. Together, let's help more kids discover the power of mindfulness!

With gratitude,
Ryuu, Kate, & **The Little Lessons of Mindfulness** Team

Made in United States
Cleveland, OH
31 May 2025

17253552R00033